NOV. 7

CHADRON STATE COLLEGE

00 89892 9

P9-CCS-810

Text copyright © 1994 by Anne Marie Linden
Illustrations copyright © 1994 by Katherine Doyle

All rights reserved. No part of this book may be reproduced or transmitted in any
form or by any means, electronic or mechanical, including photocopying,
recording, or by any information storage and retrieval stystem, without permission
in writing from the Publisher.

Atheneum
Macmillan Publishing Company
866 Third Avenue
New York, NY 10022

Macmillan Publishing Company is part of the
Maxwell Communication Group of Companies.

First U.S. edition
First published in Great Britain by Reed Children's Books

Printed in China

10 9 8 7 6 5 4 3 2 1
The text of this book is set in Stempel Garamond.
The illustrations are rendered in chalk pastel.
ISBN 0–689–31946–0

Library of Congress Catalog Card Number 94–70231

EMERALD BLUE

Anne Marie Linden
illustrated by Katherine Doyle

ATHENEUM   1994   NEW YORK
MAXWELL MACMILLAN INTERNATIONAL
New York Oxford Singapore Sydney

TA F. KING LIBRARY

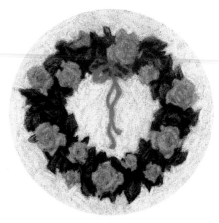

To the fond memory of my grandmother, Lillian Cox,
to my brothers and sisters Emerson, Glenn, Judy, and Lorna with love,
and for the Morning Star, Christmas Rose…and the hope of the evergreen ring…
thank you, thank you, thank you

A.M.L.

To all children everywhere,
especially those who might be sad,
the sun will shine again;
to my family,
to my Prince

K.D.

LONG AGO AND FAR AWAY, I lived with my brother and
grandmother on a coral island in the Caribbean. Our little house
stood on stilts and in our backyard we kept goats, a donkey called
Jack, and a cat that definitely had nine lives.

Growing at the front of the house were rosebushes with fat pink
flowers. On the left side stood a sour cherry tree, and on the right
was a piece of land on which Grandma grew her vegetables. We
ate good food on the island, food that you've possibly never
seen in your whole life.

There were plantains: thick like bananas, only bigger and longer, and they taste good fried like chips. We had sweet potatoes. Boy! everything on that island tasted sweet. There was guava jam and mango cheese, banana bread and rice and peas, soup with breadfruit, pumpkin and callaloo, roasted peanuts, corn and coo-coo. We drank the sticky juice of passion fruit, and sugarcane, and clear, cool water from the backyard tap. The air was sweetly spiced with the scent of cinnamon and nutmeg.

Each morning my brother Em and I would race each other to the goats' pen. Whoever reached there first was allowed to milk the goats. We would squeeze their udders and watch the creamy milk squirt and froth in the tin bucket. It was warm and sweet and tasted delicious.

After we'd collected the goat's milk, my grandma, sitting in her
rocking chair, would put me between her knees and rub coconut
oil into my hair to make it soft and shiny.

She would comb my dry curls until they were smooth and
long, and braid them into two fat plaits, tying them with
two red ribbons. Then we would leave for school.

My brother would go one way and I the other. Em was two years older than me, so he attended the big school. I would wait at the bottom of the lane for my friends, Merly and Blossom and Maimie Lee, and we would walk together. We didn't wear shoes to school,

and on some days the road was too hot for walking, so we'd hop
and skip like jackrabbits until we found some cool, lush grass to
tread on. If Banana Tree had dropped his long, smooth palm
leaves, we would step on these too.

I was always the first one
home, but one day, as
I walked along the lane,
I saw Em in the distance,
running, running like the
wind. So I ran too. By
the time I reached him,
Em was already inside

and Grandma was standing tall and straight on the veranda.
Suddenly a large black shape rose from the cherry tree and with
a loud croaking noise flew high over the house and flapped
away. I did not know what kind of bird it was, but it gave me
the shivers. I went up the steps, and Grandma and I went inside.
Em was crouched in the corner, trembling, his teeth chattering.
"A j-jumbie bird, a j-jumbie bird," he stammered.
"It w-w-watched me through my c-c-classroom window, so I ran
away and, see, it followed me home."
"Easy, chile, easy," whispered Grandma. "It gone. Come see."
Holding tight to Grandma's skirt, Em followed her onto the
veranda. The day looked normal, happy and bright. Not a
jumbie bird in sight. Grandma made a special drink from herbs
and flowers to take away our fears, and the next morning Em
didn't have to go to school, but I did. I wished it was the jumbie
bird that had chased me home.

In the evenings, we would sit out on the veranda and wait for the stars to shine. My grandma in her rocking chair would rock gently and slowly, back and forth, humming a hymn. Sometimes she'd stop and sigh, so softly, so sadly.

"Chile," she would say. I liked it when she called me chile.
It was like the soft kiss of the evening breeze.
Outside I could hear the frogs croaking and the hush
of the sea as it breathed.

My uncle Frankie was a
fisherman. He would go out
most mornings in his boat.
If my brother and I were
down on the beach,
we would catch sight of his
boat bobbing up and down on
the emerald blue water and we
would wave and shout until he saw us.

Then he would wave back and make a sign with his hand for us
to swim out to him. He sure as sure knew we could not swim, but
he liked to tease us.

One day Em stood on the shore and ran at a wave. With all his
might, he flung himself at it. It caught him and carried him a
little way, sweeping him high, dashing him low. Then folding
over him like a cloak, it rolled him back on the beach, right at
my feet. The frothing white foam bubbled over him, chuckling
merrily at his effort, and Grandma laughed too.
Later my uncle came to the house with his catch and emptied it
on the stone floor of the kitchen. The fish flopped this way and
that, twisting and turning their shiny bodies as they beat the floor
and gasped for life. Poor, poor, pretty fish.
"Chile...," Grandma sighed on the cool evening breeze.

The day the donkey and the goats in the yard were restless and
the cat kept padding up and down on the veranda, and the leaves
on the trees whispered fiercely scurry, scurry, scurry, and Grandma
scorched my new red ribbon on the hot iron, *that* day the
hurricane came.

The winds howled round our door and shook the house.

The rain beat down on the tin roof and sounded like a hundred
steel drums. Grandma took Em and me by the hand and led us
out into the wild night.

As we struggled down the lane, the wind tugged at our clothes and tried to drive us back and knock us down. On and on we pushed. There were people all around us, all running for the strong shelter that was my school. Once inside, we settled down for the night with warm blankets, feeling excited and cosy with our grandma close beside us.

For Em and me, it was an adventure. Grandma hummed her hymn and thanked the Lord for delivering us safely. Outside, the hurricane howled and wailed its fury throughout the night; banging on doors and rattling windows, it screamed through the keyhole. But we were safe and it could not reach us.

I snuggled up to Grandma and fell into a deep sleep.

The next morning the sun was up and the hurricane had gone.
Grandma said it just blew itself out. We stepped outside.
The air smelled fresh and clean, like a new beginning.
The trees leaned this way and that, and our house didn't know
how to stand, but the animals were safe and Uncle Frankie had
already started work on fixing our home. All day long we helped
him hammer nails and carry wood.

So soon, too soon after the hurricane, our mother arrived
on the island to take us away and over the sea.
I did not remember her, although Em did. She was very
beautiful and wore fancy perfume, and her nails were long
and pretty and painted red. She told us fabulous stories of

our new country – of the snow, the tiny flakes of ice like syrup
shavings, that fell from the sky in winter and covered the earth
and rooftops white. I needed to see this snow, so like lambs we
followed her.   We only wanted to see the snow, then come
straight back to Grandma.

So at the airport I did not worry very much when Grandma, holding us close and crying, softly spoke. I was so excited that I did not hear her beautiful singsong words, but I felt the sadness of them as her wet cheeks touched mine. I did not look back as we ran up the steps of the airplane.

And though I never saw her again, our grandmother left her
love in this world for us. For when I breathe in the
magic of a starry night and the evening breeze
stirs the leaves and sounds like the hush
of the sea, gently, gently, far away,
sighing softly, I hear her say,
"Chile..."